DRAMA FREAK

FROM CREATIVE VISIONAIRE

JORDAN STRAMER

STRAMER HOUSE

New York Toronto London Paris Sydney
Seoul Tokyo

This first one is for Mom and Dad, who gave me the world and
everything in it.
It will be us three until the end.
Always.
Forever.
And even after that…

WARNING!

Slasher High is a fast paced, teenage horror novel, set in 1996.

Within these pages contain horrifying imagery of murder, death, dismemberment, guts and gore, intense violence, disturbing characters, haunting environments, and blood, so much blood... Readers who may be sensitive to these elements, please be aware and prepare yourself.

Welcome to Hollow Creek High School, where students are just dying to learn...

Contents

Chapter 1

Of course I got detention on Halloween.

Why would it happen on any other day?

I mean, of all the days of the year it could happen, obviously it had to be today.

It just *had* to be.

Something like this doesn't happen on regular, boring days.

Not to mention it was only my second week at a new school, and already I was getting into trouble.

On *Halloween* of all days.

Like seriously?

The one day of the year I was looking forward to, and now I'm spending two hours in the library after school instead.

Even as the word *detention* came barging out of Mr. Evans fat mouth, I still couldn't believe it.

But it happened.

And just like that I'm stuck after school for two hours, instead of enjoying the evening like everyone else.

Believe me, this was not how I wanted to spend my Halloween.

All day I've had to listen to everyone blab about the town's annual Pumpkin Festival that happens every year on Halloween, and all day I've been getting more and more excited about that last bell so I could experience my first one.

When biology class started, I couldn't wait to hear the bell ring.

Now, as I sit here waiting for fourth period to end, I only dread the next two hours to come.

And the worst part, none of this was even my fault. I only got detention because of Reese and that dead frog…

Hang on, before I get ahead of myself, let me start from the beginning.

My name is Alex Jones, and I'm the newest junior at Hollow Creek High School.

At first my day started off great.

Driving to school was like stepping into an old classic Halloween movie.

Orange leaves, red leaves, and yellow leaves fell from the trees, blowing away on a gentle breeze, getting scattered across all the front yards in Hollow Creek.

Every house was smothered in Halloween decorations.

Fake spider webs strangled the bushes and trees, dangling from branches. Plastic skeletons rose from the ground, reaching for their next victim. One house had an inflated purple and green witch brewing a smoking cauldron, as fog bellowed over its edge. Carved pumpkins sat on porches with different glowing faces. Most were evil and sneering. A few were happy and laughing, having a fun time. One semi-rotten pumpkin had a menacing scowl with crooked mismatched eyes, a wide curved smile and sharp fangs.

When I made the turn onto the town's main street, Hollow Drive, the sun was barely rising in the pale-blue sky, and the brisk morning wind reminded me of winter's coming arrival.

It was the perfect start to Halloween.

If only it stayed like that...

When I got to school, students were scrambling in the parking lot, bundled in their jackets and hoodies, talking about Halloween plans, the costumes they planned to wear tonight, the piles of candy they planned to stuff in their faces while they watched scary movies, but most of all, they were talking about the town's annual Pumpkin Festival happening tonight.

My sneakers crunched over orange and brown leaves in the parking lot as I made my way towards the school.

My family had just moved here last month after my dad's new job, so we were still getting used to our new home, and town, but apparently the town of Hollow Creek took their holiday and non-holiday festivities very, *very* serious.

A little too serious if you ask me.

And they hold Halloween above all other holidays, which means so does the high school, and it's student inhabitants.

Don't get me wrong, I love the spooky season and trick-or-treating as much as anyone else, but when I walked into school today...

I'll admit it was a bit much.

Covered from floor to ceiling, red and black streamers sparkled in the light. Patches of paper-pumpkins lined the halls, and plastic bats dangled overhead on strings. Fake painted blood ran down classroom doors. On the walls, paper-cut-out zombies, mummies, and werewolves stared at us with wild eyes as we passed the front entrance.

The school's red lockers were already old and rusted, but with the added cobwebs strung across, abandoned was the next word on the list.

Oh, not to mention the ghosts that floated about in the halls.

That's right, my new school was haunted by *ghosts*.

Ghosts made of pillowcases and black-paper eyes.

Came to find out, it's a senior tradition to throw pillowcases over balloons and let them float aimlessly around the school, a tradition representing the graduating students moving on from the school. Most of the balloon ghosts bobbed up and down into a large huddle over the cafeteria, usually bundling in one corner of the ceiling.

And I must admit, I loved every bit of it.

I passed the door to the music room, which had a particularly gruesome looking band of ghouls, each playing their own instrument. One ghoul with long black hair and a black top hat was shredding on the guitar. Another sported an eye-patch, a gold hoop earring, and a red bandana holding a mic. The last one was a one-armed drummer who was using his other arm as a drumstick.

With a smile on my face, I made my way to first period English.

On the way I heard a lot of the younger students talking about their costumes for tonight at the festival.

Which made me think about my own plans after school.

Getting home before my parents, making a cup of hot coco, one hand in a bag of mixed candy, sitting cozy on the couch with a new book in the other hand. Then to finish it off tonight, a pizza and scary movie marathon, as is tradition.

Most of the upper-class students were consumed with the school's first home football game tomorrow, and the costume parties being thrown afterwards.

The varsity quarterback, Billy Jenkins, could be seen with his group of jocks standing against the wall of red lockers, picking on the passing freshman. His real name is William, but apparently if anyone calls him that, they get stuffed into one of those lockers.

I only knew of Billy from his reputation around the school.

He was one of the biggest players on the football team, with a chin to match it. He looked like your typical blonde hair, popular quarterback-jock in a red letterman jacket. Two letters, 'HC' were patched to the front.

As I made my way to first period, passing a group of giggling freshman girls who were exchanging looks as I passed by, that happens when you're the new kid, is when I saw Reese come bursting down the hall.

Turns out the first person I met at my new school, Reese Lowe, is the biggest class clown in school history. A hardcore geek who reads manga and listens to loud, heavy metal music during class. And who gets frequently yelled at for it.

He came strutting over with a big grin on his face and threw his arm around my shoulder.

"You ready for tonight bro?!"

"Ready for what?" I asked curiously.

"Dude, what are you talking about? It's *Halloween!* The Pumpkin Festival is today!"

"Pumpkin Festival?"

"Yeah, everyone in town goes. I like to go for the all-you-can-eat Pumpkin Pie contest."

"How many different types of pumpkin pies are there?"

"You'd be surprised. Last year the winner was Mrs. Jones, and her pumpkin-cinnamon swirl pie."

I thought of pumpkin pie the entire time we headed to first period English class.

Our substitute, Mrs. Seal, was brought in a few days before I started since the original teacher, Mr. Beverly, didn't show up for work last week.

Some say he quit. Some think he's on vacation.

Others claim he died and became a ghost who haunts the school at night.

All I know is he was a favored teacher by many students, and I never got the chance to meet him.

We walked into English class and took our seats, pulling the homework out from last night. We were tasked with writing a short ghost story, and volunteers could share with the class for extra credit.

But when no one raised their hand to go first, Mrs. Seal randomly called on someone to share.

"Let's see," she said looking at the list of students on a sheet. "How about Claire Adams?"

I didn't know much about her other than she was the girl always sketching in her notebook during class. She was the typical artsy-fartsy girl. She was shy, timid, and spent most of her time drawing.

During class, as one of our classmates was reading a ghost story, Claire Adams started screaming at the top of her lungs.

Everyone in class recoiled and jumped in their seats, covering their ears.

Her screams rang my ears and probably the entire school. When her screams died down, I noticed what she was screaming at. The brown spot on her shirt grew wings and started screeching and flying in circles around her head.

No, not a brown spot.

But a brown *vampire bat!*

The bat began circling around the classroom, sending all the girls into shrieking terror under their desks. Even the substitute, Mrs. Seal, shielded herself with a binder behind the desk, pawing at the phone trying to call the front office.

Among the screams, as we all got low below our desks, I saw the look on Reese's face and that gave me a hunch about where the bat came from and how it ended up on Claire's shirt.

Since the sub didn't have any real proof where the bat came from, even though most of her attention was on Reese for the rest of class, she was able to get the front-desk security officer down here and release the little guy safely back outside.

The security officer, an older man named Terrance, who had been working at the school for over two decades, came in with a fishing net and trash bag and was able to safely grab the little guy and set him free outside.

When the first bell sounded and we walked out of the classroom, Reese burst into hysterical laughter.

"Dude! Did you see all the girls freak out? Oh man, and the way Claire was screaming bloody murder? That was so choice!"

I tried not to laugh but I couldn't help it, even I let a smile loose.

We walked ahead a little further and then both went our separate ways.

"See you at lunch!" He said, waving as he made his way to woodshop class. "And just think about tonight."

Chapter 2

For me, second period Drama and Theater class was next. It was my only elective today, with Mr. Perkins: a gaunt, grouchy old man, with balding gray hair slicked back on each side. His face was thin and sharp. His eyes were sunken, and baggy. And he walked with a crooked demeanor that made people usually want to stay away. He also smelled like an antique store and onions.

We spent the entire class setting up props and building stage pieces for his upcoming school play: *The Phantom of the Opera*.

I was assigned to paint the wooden beams black for the stage building.

The whole time we worked, Mr. Perkins just kept hobbling around, muttering to himself in a low whisper that only he could hear.

While I was busy brushing a fresh coat of red paint on a wooden beam, one of the girls in my class, Emily Davis, who also happened to be varsity captain of the cheer-squad, and the most popular girl in school, or so Reese told me, came walking over to me as I was mid-brush.

"Hi, you're Alex, right?" her voice was light and sweet, like a summer breeze. "The new kid in town." She smiled and slid a loose strand of brown hair behind her ear.

At first, I didn't know what to say. "Uh—yeah, that's me."

"Yeah, I know, I've seen you around. So, me and the girls are throwing a costume party tomorrow night at my place. My parents are out of town. You should totally come. The party starts around nine but feel free to come whenever. Here's my address."

She handed me a small piece of folded paper, inside it was her home address scribbled in the neatest cursive I've ever seen.

"That sounds fun," I told her. "Maybe I'll stop by."

"You definitely should!" She clapped her hands and walked back over to her friend, Madison Shelby, who happened to be the second most popular girl in school. They both looked at me and started giggling in unison.

Once drama class ended with the bell, and I managed to paint several wooden beams and walls, I made my way to lunch.

I saw Reese sitting at a far table with the usual suspects, rambling on about pumpkin pie and the *Death Moon* marathon on TV tonight.

One of his friends, Robbie Fenwick, sat beside him listening intensely as he reached into his *Power Rangers* lunchbox. He opened the lid and pulled out a sandwich wrapped in plastic. Once unwrapped, he took a huge bite.

He chewed for a moment or two, then his eyes went wide with terror, and he had a confused look across his face. "What the—!"

The confusion turned to horror when his sandwich started *moving*.

One of the boys next to Robbie hollered, "Woah! Look! It's come alive!"

I looked down at the twitching sandwich, and saw several, thin brown fingers poking out of the bread, reaching for him.

I couldn't believe it…

His sandwich was alive!

And had grown *fingers*!

Chapter 3

Long brown fingers wiggled and squirmed from in between the bread.

"My sandwich is alive! It's a zombie sandwich!" Robbie screamed.

We all took a closer look, and noticed the gnarled fingers weren't zombie fingers.

But instead, thick slimy *worms*.

Brown worms squirming between the lettuce and tomato struggling to break free.

Robbie's face turned a sickly green. He shot up from the table and ran towards the bathroom, both hands clutched over his mouth.

None of us thought he would make it back.

I looked over at Reese who was enjoying a similar looking sandwich to Robbie's, wrapped in plastic wrap.

"Wait, did you—"

"Me and Rob have second period together. Switched it out when he wasn't looking. He made way too easy."

We spent the rest of lunch talking about Halloween and what were the scariest movies to watch on Halloween, while Robbie spent the rest of it in the bathroom.

When he finally came back and sat down at the table, his face was pale and flushed, but he had a wide grin across his face.

I figured he would be furious with Reese, but according to everyone at the table, this was a known tradition that every Halloween, Reese, liked to pull pranks, or 'tricks', as he calls them, on unsuspecting students.

Even his friends.

To them, it was considered a great honor to be the victim of one of his infamous pranks.

Can you believe that?

They rattled off a few of his pranks from previous years. Exploding pumpkins. Slime filled balloons. Rats in the girls locker room. Okay, that one is funny. But this is what he does. He's a trickster. The town clown.

But he didn't seem to care. In his own way, Reese was a leper and proud of it.

Once lunch was over, we made our way to third period.

Gym class.

This is where Halloween really started to take a turn for the worst.

Gym class began as usual.

We changed into our shirts and shorts in the locker rooms and began stretching and warming up on the basketball courts. The wooden floors were freshly mopped so every few seconds you'd hear a high squeak from sneakers skidding on the court.

Coach Carter eventually came over, blew his whistle, and announced that we would be playing dodgeball today and divided us up into four teams. A mix of girls and boys, juniors and sophomores.

During the first match, my team was up against Billy Jenkins' team, and for some reason unknown, I swear he was coming for me.

Every throw he made was targeted at me. He didn't throw at anyone else.

I finally was able to dodge one of his throws and counter him with a quick distraction. I threw one ball high up for him to catch and then chucked another ball I grabbed off the ground right into his gut before the other ball landed in his arms.

He was out. I got him. Everyone on my team screamed and cheered as Billy slunk off to the sidelines.

Shortly after I got hit by one of his buddies who seemed to carry out his mission until I was tagged. The ball barely grazed my leg.

Even after an hour of playing and watching different teams battle it out with red dodgeballs, and multiple bloody noses, Billy was still staring at me with fire in his eyes.

Coach Carter blew his final whistle ending the games.

It was time to clean up and get ready before the next bell.

While we were all standing near the doors of the gym waiting for the bell, after changing in the locker rooms, someone shouted behind me.

"Hey, new kid!"

I turned to see Billy Jenkins barging towards me. His teeth were bare and his eyes narrow as he walked up to me. He wasn't much taller, maybe a few inches, but now it seemed like a few feet.

He leaned close to my face. I could smell strong minty-gum breath in each word he spoke.

"Heard you were flirting with my girlfriend earlier."

"What?" I didn't expect that.

"Are you deaf?" He snorted. "Someone told me they saw you flirting with Emily. I don't know what you think you're doing but stay the hell away from her."

"I have no idea what you're talking about! Whoever told you that is a liar. She approached me. She invited me. That's all."

He leaned closer. His eyes were on fire. "She invited you to her party?" He seemed surprised by that.

"Look man, I didn't even know she was going to. She came up to me first."

"I don't care. All I know is someone left a note in my locker saying you were. Look, I don't want you to talk to her. I don't want you to look at her. Just stay away from her. And if you show up to her party, you're going to regret it."

"Wait, a note? Billy I wasn't trying anything. I swear she came up to me and—"

Billy's face turned red hot, and his hands balled into fists.

"You don't want to mess with—"

Wham!

Before he could finish his sentence, his face twisted and recoiled as he fell to the ground.

Bouncing off his head and rolling away was a red dodgeball.

When we looked over to see who threw it, Reese was howling with laugher and pointing at Billy, holding more dodgeballs under his arm. All the other students started to join in on the laughter.

"Bullseye!" Reese cheered. "Or should I say *Billyseye!*"

"Reese you little—"

Wham!

Another dodgeball nailed the side of his head.

Billy got up roaring and ran at Reese like a madman.

"I'm going to—!"

Wham!

Another ball to the face.

"You're dead loser!"

Finally, the bell sounded and the last thing I saw was Billy chasing after Reese, both disappearing into the large crowd of students flooding into the hallway.

At some point Reese must have lost Billy, because seconds later he came running up next to me, sweating and out of breath.

"Thanks for the save," I told him. "But you know he's probably going to kill you now."

"He can try. Anyway, we still on for tonight?"

"I never agreed to that."

"Come on dude! It's the entire *Dread Moon* series. All five movies, including—"

"Including the extended cuts of each film and behind the scenes footage. How could I forget when you've told me a thousand times already."

"So that means you're down?"

I didn't answer.

Instead, I ignored him and kept walking to the next class, and he started ranting about a manga series he's currently nose-deep in.

At the end of the hall, I saw Emily and Madison standing with their posse of cheerleaders.

They all seemed to be watching me as I walked by.

Madison whispered something into Emily's ear and they both giggled. Behind her, Billy and his boys walked up and joined them.

I wondered who left that note about me flirting with Emily? Why would someone do that?

We arrived in the science hall a moment later and walked into fourth period Biology class.

When I entered the room, my eyes went wide.
My stomach turned at the smell of decaying flesh.
And I could see why.
The entire room was filled with dead bodies.

Chapter 4

On each black-top table, sprawled out on metal trays, were large, green, dead bodies.

Dead *frog* bodies.

They all stared up at the ceiling with milky, lifeless eyes.

Sitting behind his desk, dressed in a blood-spattered white lab-coat and wearing a surgical mirror band around his head, was Mr. Elchinco. Beads of fake blood ran down his neck.

According to Reese, only grade-grubbers liked Mr. Elchinco. Everyone else said he was mean and too strict. He was a stick of man, no more than thirty. He wore glasses on top of his long, snobby nose, and his beady little eyes, black as ink, were always looking down on someone. He was the type of person to correct your mistake in front of the whole class to make you feel embarrassed.

Once we all took our seats, Mr. Elchinco cleared his throat and stood up. "Today we are having our frog dissections. This, as you know, will count as a test grade. You and your partner will have the remainder of class to harvest the organs listed on the sheet, place them in their corresponding labeled jars, and write a brief description of each organ's functionality."

"Wicked!" Reese shouted. "It's about time we did something cool in his class."

"We should be dissecting you freak," Billy said, laughing with his partner, Marcus Brown.

I haven't officially met Marcus yet, but I've seen him around school. He usually hangs out with Billy's crew. He was always walking around school with headphones on, listening to music and writing lyrics in a journal. He was popular among the school for having a dad who was a famous jazz player, a local legend to Hollow Creek. He always had the freshest kicks on, and the hippest outfits.

Most of the popular kids did it seemed.

Mr. Elchinco ignored the comment and shot Reese with a warning glare. "This is not playtime—as I must remind you—we are dealing with razor sharp utensils and toxic chemicals. Any fooling around will not be tolerated. *At all.*"

His eyes lingered on Reese as he spoke. The silence in the room lingered for a few seconds.

"I will come around and check on each table's progress. You have until the end of class to turn in your organ jars. Okay, you may begin."

We all started putting on our plastic gloves and safety goggles.

I looked at Reese. "You want to cut first?"

"No, you go ahead. I've got a better idea."

Twenty minutes in and the sound of scalpels and tweezers clinking against each other filled the room. Organs were being placed in jars, being shuffled and rearranged. Everyone was busy harvesting tiny organs from the frogs and making scrunched-up faces as they did it.

Everyone except Reese.

Mr. Elchinco was hovering at the front table, leaning over and checking on two students I didn't know. He didn't seem pleased with their work.

I turned to look at the other tables to my right, to check their progress, and to make sure I wasn't butchering my frog worse than I was.

When I turned back to the table, my frog was gone!

I scanned the table. The floor. The ceiling. My frog was nowhere to be seen.

Great, now they're turning into zombie frogs.

And that's when I saw Reese.

And I saw what he was holding.

Where he was holding it.

And who he was holding it at.

"Hey Emily," Reese said, holding the green frog corpse with both hands, "kiss my frog and maybe it'll turn into your prince charming."

"Ew! Get away freak! I'd *rather* kiss that dead frog than you." She said backing up into her chair.

He raised the frog and dangled in front of her face; part of its intestines was hanging out like tiny pale strings. "That can be arranged."

It happened so fast I couldn't have stopped it if I wanted to, and for some reason, part of me didn't want to.

Billy leaned across his table. "Reese get that thing away from her or I swear your dead."

Mr. Elchinco shouted from the front of the class. "That's enough, now knock it off!"

Reese ignored everyone.

"Come on Emily, froggy just wants a kiss from the prettiest girl in school!" He said dangling the frog closer. And closer. And closer.

Her face twisted in disgust. "Stop Reese! Get that nasty—"

When she opened her mouth again, the frog went in.

"Hole in one!" Reese cheered, raising a fist in the air. "There you go Billy, just did you a favor my good man."

The frog's limp legs dangled back and forth, making the frog appear as if it was dancing.

Emily tried screaming but only a muffled groan came out.

In her sudden panic she elbowed the table behind her, knocking the jars of organs off the desk, sending them crashing to the ground.

Pieces of glass shattered, and tiny organs scattered everywhere.

A tiny frog brain bounced under our table and bumped into my shoe.

Sitting next to Billy listening to music, Marcus jumped out of his chair nearly hitting his head on the ceiling.

"YO! My shoes!" He said lifting his feet off the ground and scanning his feet. He looked furious. "Reese, you dumb mother—!"

Marcus grabbed the frog from his tray by the leg and flung it at Reese's head.

Reese, who was busting out laughing on the brink of tears, dodged the frog at the last second, and we watched it fly across the room, hitting Mr. Elchinco square in the face.

The frog slowly peeled off his face leaving slimy strings behind.

All the laughter in the room dropped like a dead fly. The tension could have been cut with a knife.

Mr. Evans' face flashed with red hot anger.

"Alright that's it!" He roared. "I've had enough! Reese—Marcus—both of you—detention! Same goes for you Billy!

"HA!" Emily snapped at Reese, "Serves you right freak."

"And Ms. Davis you can join them!"

"Wait what?!" Emily had tears swelling in her eyes.

"That's not fair!" Billy protested.

Marcus pointed at us. "Reese is the one—!"

"Not another word or I'll make it today and tomorrow!" His tone was cold and sharp like a razor. "And if any of you skip detention, I'll make sure you have detention every Friday for the rest of the year! Now clean your mess up. The rest of you," he turned back to the class, "finish your assignment— in silence!"

No one moved. No one said a word.

They were all staring at me.

I hadn't realized I was still laughing until Mr. Elchinco was standing over me, his eyes like beady daggers into my soul. On his face, just below his eyes, little chunks of frog intestine dangled from his cheek.

Truth be told, it was hard not to laugh.

"Find something funny Mr. Jones?" His sudden sarcastic change in voice sent a chill down my back. "I would think as the new student, you would want to put your best foot forward. But since you find it so funny, you can join your Reese in detention as well."

And just like that, I had detention.

All because of Reese and that stupid frog.

We spent the rest of the class in silence, cleaning up our table area, and turning in what was left of the assignment, what we could manage at least. I was able to find a tiny frog brain that had been sent flying from Billy's table.

I picked up the brain near my foot, placing it in the corresponding labeled jar and watched Marcus spend the rest of the class searching the ground for it.

Towards the end, I turned in the rest of our organs. Hopefully we can get a decent grade on it for our troubles, anything above failing at this point is better than nothing.

Once the class was about to end, everyone started turning in organ jars and packing their bags in silence, while waiting for the bell.

When it finally sounded, everyone in class bursted out of the room filled with excitement for a Halloween filled evening. Everyone will be heading to the Pumpkin Festival at 3pm.

Everyone except us.

On our way out the door, I had to ask Reese the obvious question.

"Did you really have to shove the frog in her mouth?" I waited for an answer as we made our way to the library.

He shrugged. "Hey, she's been asking for it. All she ever does is pick on me, along with her buffoon of a boyfriend."

As we were leaving the science hall, Billy jerked his shoulder into mine and spoke through clenched teeth, in a whisper only we could hear. *"Watch yourself newbie. One way or another, you and Reese are dead."*

Billy walked away and caught up with Emily.

Emily was still trying to clean her mouth, scratching at her tongue, shoving pieces of minty gum in her mouth. She didn't say anything to anyone on the way out. She just wanted to go to the bathroom and clean herself up.

A part of me felt bad...

But not my girlfriend, so not my problem.

We passed Marcus, who was standing at his locker changing his socks, wiping organ juices off his shoe with a clean rag. I think he cared more about his new shoes than the detention. But as we walked past him, even he shot us a death stare.

It was when I saw Emily run into the bathroom, seeming on the verge of tears, that I started to really feel bad.

Maybe it wasn't so funny after all.

"She should try using a dirty sock or some duct tape." Reese said as we made our way to the library, instead of outside, towards the student parking lot like everyone else.

"You shouldn't have done that. It wasn't cool." I told him watching the rush of students bursting out the doors, heading to the parking lot.

"I didn't do it because I thought it was a nice and safe thing to do. I did it because she deserved it."

"For what?"

Reese's face shifted in a way I hadn't seen it before. His eyes narrowed in suspicion. His upper lip twitched. And his words were ice cold. "Don't worry about it."

Reese walked the rest of the way in silence.

We split from the large herd of students heading towards the parking lot, watching them bound off with excitement for the Halloween festival, trick-or-treating, and haunted trails. All the stuff I probably wouldn't get to do now.

I had to get out of here. Maybe there was a way I could get off detention early.

You know, act nicely to Ms. Barnes. Try to explain how this was all just a big misunderstanding. Maybe I could play the new kid card, and she'll feel bad for me.

Yeah, probably not.

Thanks to my friend Reese, I now have the reputation of troublemaker by association.

"Let's get this over with," Reese said as we turned into the short hall leading to the library, "if we're lucky, Ms. Barnes—she's in charge of detention—will let us go early and we can still catch the *Death Moon* marathon."

I ignored the last part. "Let's just hope I can still go to Emily's party tomorrow—if she doesn't already hate me thanks to you."

"Wait, you're actually going to that?"

"Well yeah," I admitted. "Why wouldn't I?"

"Because she's a snobby rich girl who thinks she's queen of the school, and everyone in it."

"Or maybe she's just misunderstood," I said optimistically. "You should be able to relate."

"No, I'm what's known as an outcast," he reminded me. "The lonely hero who ends up saving the day—despite the ridicule of his peers. A *leper* if you will. One of a kind which means no one can replace the masterpiece that is, Reese."

"Alright, *masterpiece*, try not to explode." I stopped in front of the double-wooden doors of the library. "Oh, and please try not to stick any dead animals in anyone's mouth. At least not while I'm around, okay?"

He gave a half-cocked smile. "No promises."

Before we entered the library, I turned to Reese one last time.

"Seriously Reese, no more pranks man. No more bats. No more worms. No more dead frogs. Let's just get this detention over with and get out of here."

"Ha! You thought those were bad?" he reached into his backpack and pulled out a mason jar.

A mason jar filled with *black spiders*.

Thick, round spiders with long thin legs, crawling over each other in a frenzy.

"Wait until you see my next trick."

Chapter 5

I convinced Reese to put the jar of spiders away before anyone noticed, so long as I promised to watch the *Death Moon* marathon with him at my house after the Pumpkin Festival.

I didn't know exactly what his plan was, but something told me it had to do with Billy and those spiders crawling inside his varsity jacket.

We didn't see Ms. Barnes, the librarian, right away.

She was probably in her office, just to the right of the double doors, near the entrance.

Her office was dark, with only a single lamp in the corner, barely illuminating her sitting at her desk.

One girl was already sitting here, Claire Adams, or 'artsy fartsy' as Reese liked to call her. I'd seen her earlier in English class.

"She's always drawing in her sketchbook. I tried taking it from her one-time last year, and she started crying for ten minutes straight until I gave it back."

"Maybe you shouldn't take things that don't belong to you."

"Or maybe people should stop leaving their things out for me to take."

Other than Claire, the library is empty. She was sitting at one of the wooden tables in the main reading area. It was hard to believe a girl like her could get detention.

A door opened behind us and the librarian came walking out of her office.

"Take your seats. Detention starts at two-thirty. It ends at four-thirty. Two hours no talking."

"Will do." I assured her.

"No worries, Miss B." Reese said winking at her. She simply rolled her eyes and continued scanning barcodes at the checkout desk.

We each took a seat at separate wooden tables, adjacent to Claire.

The library doors burst open, and a voice roared.

"Reese you owe me some new shoes!"

I turned to see a tall, lanky, brown kid, listening to music. I recognized his corn-rowed hair, his diamond stud earrings, and his wide bright smile of perfect teeth from biology class. Marcus Brown came over to where we were sitting and stared down over our tables.

"Don't worry Reese. Once we get out of here, me and Billy will make sure you get home safely."

"You touch me, and you'll wish you hadn't." Reese said, reaching into his backpack and flashed Marcus the mason jar inside.

Marcus's eyes went wide. "I swear if you—"

"*Shhhhh!*" The librarian shushed from behind the checkout counter. She held a forefinger to her mouth.

Marcus whispered under his breath. *"We'll finish this later."*

Marcus took his seat at the table across from ours.

He leaned next to Claire. "Artsy-fartsy? What are you doing here?"

Claire angled her sketchbook for him to see.

"Got in trouble for drawing in class again," she said not taking her eyes off her sketchbook. "Wow these are actually pretty good." Marcus told her, smiling with his pearly whites.

"Thanks," she said shyly. "But their just sketches."

Reese, who was listening in, leaned back in his chair and looked over his shoulder to see her drawings. "Where are the hands? None of your sketches have hands."

"Hands are harder for me to draw. I'm still learning so that's why I'm always practicing."

"Well keep it up," Marcus said. "You got talent. That's more than most can say." He shot Reese another glare.

Claire blushed.

Reese laughed. "Looks like you got yourself a new girlfriend Marcus."

"Shut up Reese."

"I second that!" A voice spoke from behind.

Billy and Emily came walking up to the other two empty tables and took their seats.

He shot Reese with a warning glare.

"Don't think I forgot what happened freak-o. When we get out of here, you're dead meat."

"Or maybe you will be." Reese reached for his backpack to grab the jar, but I grabbed his arm before he could make the situation any worse.

"Remember our deal?" I reminded him.

"Er, yeah I remember," he grumbled. He stuck his tongue out at Billy and turned around.

Emily was still quiet. She seemed too embarrassed to look at anyone or speak. Once she looked at me, and when I thought I would see pure loathing hatred, it was the opposite.

She seemed sad.

Does she want me to apologize for what he did? I thought. *What would I have to be sorry for?*

"Detention starts now," the librarian informed us a moment later. Sure enough, the clock struck two-thirty on the dot. "Two hours. No talking." Ms. Barnes went back into her office and closed the door.

With that, we all exchanged our final glances at each other, and settled into our two-hour silent treatment.

Everyone was in their own world. Billy laid his head down to go to sleep. Emily was checking her makeup, filing her nails. Marcus was listening to music and scribbling words in his notebook. Claire was drawing in her sketchbook; her pencil went in all directions as her eyes never left the paper.

Reese seemed to be the only one waiting for something. Or someone.

Waiting for what, or who, I didn't want to know.

Instead, I took out my homework for tomorrow's classes and began studying.

Only a few minutes passed, and already my eyes felt heavy. I could feel my mind nodding in and out. I laid my head down on the cool, wooden surface for just a moment, and nodded off to sleep.

That's when I woke up to a blood chilling scream.

Chapter 6

I scanned the area to find the source of the scream and watched in horror as a girl was getting brutally mauled by a yeti.

Yeah, brutally mauled on a television screen in an old 80's horror film.

Playing on the TV sitting on a rolling cart near the chalk board, was a cheesy movie scene showing a gruesome scene of a young teenage girl getting attacked by a large, yeti-like snow monster.

I looked at Reese. "How did you—?

"Not my first detention," he said grinning, holding an empty VHS box in his hand. The title read: *Night of the Snow Beast*. "She always stays in her office during detention. Usually doesn't come out until the end, so I make sure to carry a spare movie for such occasions."

Speaking of which, I checked the clock and to my dismay, we still had forty minutes left in detention.

I jumped when a door closed in the library. I spun around.

No one was there, and no one seemed to be coming or going.

I looked over at the librarian's office. Her door was closed, the blinds were shut so you couldn't see inside the windows.

Strange. Why would she shut her blinds?

Since I didn't have much time left, and I didn't feel like watching the rest of the cheesy eighties movie, I shuffled up my homework and resumed studying where I left off.

Detention went smoothly for the remainder of time.

It was quiet, albeit a little too quiet at times, but as the clock hands showed ten minutes till four-thirty, there was still no sign of Miss Barnes.

She knew detention ended soon. Right?

She wasn't going to keep us here even longer. Not on Halloween. Right?

Dread came over me, but as I watched the big-hand land on the six, marking the end of detention, all of us were confused when we didn't see the librarian come out to release us.

"She knows it ends at four-thirty, right?" Billy said to no one in particular.

"Maybe she's taking a nap?" Emily suggested.

"A nap, right now?" Marcus snorted.

"Well, she is like a hundred years old," Reese snickered.

"Shut up Reese, if it wasn't for you, we wouldn't even be in this mess." Marcus pointed out.

Something didn't seem right.

"Could she really be napping?" I asked Reese. "Maybe we should check on her."

"You losers do what you want, I'm out of here," said Billy slinging his backpack over his shoulder. "We served our time, no reason to stay any longer."

Billy got up and walked past the librarian's office, over to the double doors, but when he grabbed the handle and pulled, he had no success.

The door didn't budge.

"What the—" he tried pulling again, and again, harder and harder, and still the doors wouldn't budge. "Alright Reese, if this is one of you little pranks you better knock it off and open these damn doors."

"You're kidding right?" Reese chuckled. "You think I would lock myself in here with you, of all people—on Halloween? Ha, that's a good one Billy Bob."

Billy stepped towards Reese, but Emily got in his way.

"Enough Billy, leave him alone. Let's just get out of here so I can go home and shower."

"And how are we supposed to do that, huh? The doors are locked shut."

"Go in her office and ask if we can go home, wake her up if you have to."

I peeked inside the wide window.

The blinds made it hard to see, but I could barely make out a lamp on the desk, giving the only light, and the dark outline of Ms. Barnes sitting in her chair, the back of her head facing us.

"Just let me do it," said Reese trying to open the door. He twisted the knob left and right, but it wouldn't budge. "Hm. That's weird."

"What?" I wondered.

"It's locked from the inside." Reese kept trying to open the door.

"What?"

"Why would she lock herself in?"

"Maybe she didn't." Reese suggested.

"Okay guys, this is starting to freak me out. Can we just find someone to let us out?" Claire said looking worried.

"How do we do that? You plan on drawing us an escape hatch?" Reese said, still trying to open the door.

"Look out everyone, I got an idea," declared Billy, backing up from the door.

"That's a first," said Reese.

"Shut up Reese. You got us into this, and I'm getting us out of here!"

He reared back and charged at the door. Throwing all his weight into it.

The door gave in and collapsed with ease. Billy lay on the floor, got up and brushed himself off. "Sorry about the door Ms. B."

One by one we entered her office, standing around her desk.

She didn't turn around. She didn't say anything. She didn't make a single noise.

No way she's still asleep after that.

"Miss Barnes?" Emily said. "We finished detention."

"Yeah, can we go home? It's past four-thirty." Marcus reminded her.

"And some of us have better things to—"

I jabbed Reese in the ribs.

"Ow—I mean, were sorry for how we behaved. We won't do it again." That was a total lie. The whole time he said that he was grinning ear to ear.

We all waited for a response.

And waited.

But Ms. Barnes didn't say a word. She didn't spin around. She didn't move. She was still as a statue.

I reached out and grabbed the back of her chair and spun her around slowly into the small shell of lamplight.

And when we saw her bloody corpse, we all cried out in horror.

Chapter 7

Billy held Emily as she screamed. Claire covered her eyes. Marcus backed up hands raised. Reese looked oddly excited, as if it was a Hollywood prop-body from one of his favorite horror films.

I was confused.

Freaked out but confused.

No one spoke at first.

We were all too stunned.

"We need to call the police," I said, picking up the phone on her desk. I pressed it to my ear and started dialing 9-1-1 but I realized there was no dial tone. I looked down and traced the phone cord and felt a cut loose end in my hand.

"Someone cut the phone cord."

"What?"

"Look," I told her. "See for yourself."

They all glanced at the cord and saw it was cut in half.

"This is just some trick or something, right? She isn't really dead...right?" Emily said, shielding herself into Billy.

It was hard to look at her. I've never seen a body look like this.

Her gray hair was messy and matted in dark red. Her clothes were ripped, punctured, and stained with blood. Not fake blood. Real blood. Her eyes were gone. Nothing but empty black sockets staring back at me. Her nose had been sliced off leaving an exposed septum. A rolled-up newspaper had been shoved halfway down her throat, and sticking proudly out of her chest, caked with blood, were a pair of scissors. And on the wall behind her, dripping to the floor, large words written in blood:

I AM WAITING…

Emily kept sobbing. "M-Miss Barnes?"

"Is she really—"

"Dead? Looks like it Sherlock," said Reese sarcastically.

"It's worse than that." I told him.

"She's been murdered." Claire finished for me.

"Exactly."

"I think I'm gonna be sick." Marcus said retching over the trash can.

"How do you know that?" Billy turned to me.

"She obviously didn't do this to herself," I told him. I began examining the body. I was being extra careful not to touch anything. "Okay, this is seriously weird."

"You're just now realizing this?" Billy asked.

"What I mean is—first the library doors are locked, so were forced to bust down this door to where we find our librarian dead in her own office, the phone cord cut, and a message written in blood…" I looked around the library. "Did you guys see anyone else come into the library over the past two hours?"

They exchanged weary glances at each other.

"Nope." Reese said, still goggling at the dead body.

"Not me." Emily sobbed.

"I was asleep," said Billy rubbing the back of his head.

"I was busy drawing in my sketchbook," said Claire, "but I never heard anyone else come in."

"I had music in, so I wouldn't of heard anything." Marcus insured us. "What's your point, new kid?"

"You can call me Alex—but my *point* is—someone is obviously doing this to us."

"But why?"

"Who would do something this messed up?"

"My money is on Reese," said Billy. "This seems like something he would do."

"Billy, I know it might be hard to process this with your *pee-brain*," retorted Reese, "but I was serving detention just like you guys. How could I pull this off?"

"Maybe you're working with someone else on this." Billy turned back to me.

"Billy enough, this isn't helping," said Emily.

"Alright, for real, who could have done this?" Marcus asked.

"Maybe it was him," said Claire. Her eyes were wide open, and she was shaking as she raised her finger, pointing towards the double doors behind us.

We turned around to see a person standing on the other side of the doors.

Only it wasn't really a person.

It was like something out of a horror movie.

A tall dark figure, draped in all black, with long black, tangled hair drooping down, staring at us with...*two faces*.

The hair on my arms and neck raised. My stomach tightened.

Two white faces side-by-side, staring at us with jagged black eyes and gaping black mouths.

Two faces I will never forget.

The left-side face was evil and happy with a menacing smile. The right-side face was angry and sad, frowning with black tears streaming down it's white, cracked face.

One happy face. One sad face. One smiling. One frowning.

The two-faced freak stood still. Staring at us.

Seconds passed, then he slowly cocked one head to the side. Then slowly tilted the other face. As if giving each one a good look at us. The dark figure raised a bladed hand from inside his black caped cloak, revealing a black-and-white striped shirt underneath.

He dragged a bladed hand, black as night, down the door, scratching into the window surface. He let his fingers linger, as he slowly stepped away from the door, still facing us, he backed away and silently disappeared around the hall.

For a moment, no one said a word.

Billy ran over to the double-doors. "What the freak was that?"

"Better question is *who* the freak was that?"

"Did you see those two faces?"

"Yeah, it looked like the drama faces, comedy and tragedy, only way more twisted." Claire pointed out.

"Okay, so who do we think this, *Drama Freak*, is?"

"Probably one of Reese's stupid friends playing a prank." Billy ran and grabbed Reese by the shirt-collar. "I swear if you have anything to do with this, I'm going to beat your—."

"Get off me!" Reese shouted, pushing off Billy. "Use your small brain Billy-Bob! Why would I want to be stuck in here with you jerks on Halloween?"

"Well, we're only in this mess because you—"

I stood in front of Reese before Billy could run his fist across his face. I wasn't as big as he was, but I was nearly as tall.

"Billy, chill out man!" Marcus must of had the same thought because he stood in front of Billy blocking him. "As much as its Reese's fault, were in this mess together and I don't think he did it."

"Besides, its Halloween," Emily pointed out. "Probably just a freshman messing around. Wouldn't be the first time." She shot Reese a look.

"Since when does murder count as a fun innocent prank? I bet Reese—"

"Reese didn't have anything to do with this. And I don't know who, or *what* that was, but I know one thing for certain," I said looking at all of them. "Whoever this Drama Freak is, it's waiting for us."

"Waiting for what?" Claire asked, half-hidden behind Marcus.

I looked back at the bloody message on the wall, above Ms. Barnes' body.

"Showtime."

Chapter 8

"Okay, screw this I'm getting out of here," said Billy grabbing a chair.

"Billy you can't—"

"Under the circumstances babe, I think I can."

Marcus raised his hand. "I second that. I say we get the hell out of here."

Billy grabbed the chair by its legs and heaved it at the double doors.

The window shattered, sending shards of glass all over the carpet.

He placed his jacket over the window frame, still edged with glass bits, sticking up like shark teeth.

"We should go tell Principal Turner," Claire whispered. She looked terrified.

"You guys can do whatever you want," said Billy helping Emily across over the window. "But I'm not staying in here for one more second with that freak running around."

Everyone climbed across the broken window in a single file. Each time, bits of glass crunched under our steps. I took one last look at Ms. Barnes.

Was there really a killer in the school? Is this really happening?

Once we were out of the library, standing in the hall, we peeked around each corner to see if the coast was clear. Most of the lights were still on, but there didn't seem to be anyone around.

"We need to go find principal Turner. He can help."

"For all we know, he's the killer."

Billy burst through the stairwell doors, heading for the exit doors.

When he went to push open the doors to go outside, nothing happened. Billy kept pushing on it, driving his shoulder harder and harder, but it didn't give.

"Marcus, give me a hand."

They both took a few steps back and charged the door.

They each drove their shoulders into the door, with all their weight behind it.

There was a THUD! and both bounced off the door with no success.

The doors were sealed shut.

Looking closer and I noticed something weird.

I walked past Billy and Marcus who were clutching their shoulders.

The locks, hinges, and door jams all had a milky-white, thick substance coated inside it.

"What is it?" Emily asked.

"I don't know," I told her. "But it kind of looks like—"

"Super glue," said Reese taking a quick glance.

"How would you know that?"

"I've used it to stick my fingers together enough times to know what it looks like."

"Funny that you just happen to know what it is."

"Think what you want, but I want to get out of here just as much as you guys."

"It doesn't matter. Whether we like it or not, we seem to be stuck in here."

"Drama Freak couldn't have sealed all the doors shut. Could he?" Claire asked.

"Drama Freak?" I questioned.

"Yeah, that's what he looks like. Unless you got a better name for that monster?"

"How about the *Phantom Freak*?" Marcus suggested.

We all looked at each other.

"Drama Freak it is." Reese said.

"Okay, lets go check to see if all the doors are locked.

Sure enough, minutes later we checked more doors down the hall. They were locked and sealed shut with super glue and zip ties.

Still no sign again of Drama Freak. But my gut told me we were still being watched.

There was no escape. We were trapped here.

Could this really be a prank? Maybe Reese took one of his pranks too far this time.

Then the sight of Ms. Barnes bloody face flashed in my mind, telling me otherwise.

Reese would never kill anyone. He couldn't have done this.

Someone was behind this.

"This can't be happening."

"We can keep checking all the doors, but I promise you they are all sealed shut. This isn't random. Whoever this *Drama Freak* is, this is all part of their plan."

"So, what do we do?"

"We need to find a way to contact the police."

"We should go see Principal Turner too, he can help."

"I'll go see if the security guard is around. The more people on our side the better."

"No, I think we should stick together."

"We don't have time. We need to get to a phone that works before—"

We all fell silent. There was noise coming from somewhere in the school.

"Do you guys hear that or am I tripping?" Marcus wondered.

We all went silent and listened closely.

"No, I hear it."

"Me too."

"Is that what I think it is?"

Echoing down the hall, from the auditorium, was the eruption of people cheering with applause.

"Is that coming from the theater?"

"Who cares, people are people, and they can help!"

"Maybe Mr. Perkins is in there rehearsing?"

"Worth a shot! At this point, anyone is better than no one."

We ran down the hall as fast as we could, bursting through the doors into the main auditorium.

"I got a bad feeling about this," I said as we burst through the theater doors.

We saw people sitting in their seats, cheering and yelling.

Only, the weren't cheering. Or clapping.

In fact, the people weren't moving at all. They sat in their seat still as statues.

But that wasn't the strange part.

Their heads were twisted around, facing away from their bodies.

They stared at us with faceless expressions.

Mannequins.

Watching us.
Waiting for us.

Chapter 9

All the people cheering, weren't cheering, or clapping. In fact, they weren't moving at all.

Dozens of mannequins were scattered among the theater seats staring at us.

The cheering and clapping were coming from somewhere else.

The speakers in the auditorium.

I looked up and found the source along the far ceiling, above the stage, speakers along the high ceiling, hidden in darkness.

Wait...those aren't living people!

"Are those, mannequins?" Emily asked.

I couldn't believe it! They *are* mannequins!

A dozen or more sitting in the seats, with blank expressions on their faces.

Then the sounds of cheering and applause stopped.

The crackle of the speakers shut off.

The room fell silent.

All the mannequin faces continued watching us with menacing grins.

My stomach felt uneasy. Something wasn't right about this.

"Do you think Mr. Perkins is doing all this?" Claire said shaking, standing behind Marcus.

"Maybe," Emily said looking around. "He is the drama teacher, plus he's old and smelly."

"What does him being smelly have to do with anything?" Reese wondered.

"I don't know, but he always smells like cooked cabbage and old antiques."

"Plus, he does hate Halloween."

"So? I doubt that old man—"

Loud static crackled through the air.

Through the speakers overhead came a static, high-pitched, raspy voice.

"Welcome everyone to the big show!"

Towards the front stage, a mechanical whirring stirred the air as the large red stage curtain began to recoil into itself on both sides, revealing the wooden stage.

The big red curtains came to a bundled halt, and hanging over the center of the stage, was a large dark mass suspended by what looked like ropes.

A spotlight beamed over center stage revealing the large mass, and hanging from the rafters by rope, dangling over center stage, was a limp body, hanging like a butchered deer, pink intestines spewed out from his stomach down to the floor.

It was Mr. Perkins. He was dead.

Emily screamed so close to my ear I thought it had ruptured.

"Are you guys seeing this right now or am I tripping?" Marcus said rubbing his hands on his head, as he started pacing back and forth.

"This is seriously messed up."

"This is like straight out of a horror movie." Reese said walking down the main isle, passing several staring mannequins.

"Shut up Reese!" Billy yelled.

"Who could do something like this." Emily wondered, tears streaming down her cheeks.

"Obviously that two headed freak-monster."

"My money is still on frog-boy over here." Billy said, walking up to Reese's face.

"Reese has nothing to do with this. Leave him alone." I told him, holding my ground firm. As much as I hated murder, I disliked bullies all the same.

"Or what new kid? What are you going to do?"

"You know Billy, I had bullies like you at my last school. And you know what I learned? Is that it's usually all talk and no action. Just a mouth spewing air."

"You want to see action new kid?"

Emily stepped in and blocked Billy from raising his clenched fists and decking me.

I wasn't scared of Billy, at all.

But I also didn't think getting into a brawl while a killer is on the prowl was the best idea right now.

"Right now, let's just focus on getting out of here and finding help." I told them, heading for the doors. "Come on, we need to find principal Turner."

Chapter 10

We burst into the principal's office a minute later only to find the principal missing.

"Great, Principal Turner is gone too."

"You don't think—"

"That he might be the killer? At this point I believe anyone is."

"I don't think so. His briefcase is still here, and his coat. Maybe he just stepped out."

"Or maybe he's running around killing people and we're all sitting ducks."

We started to search through his desk when someone appeared at the doorway.

"What do you kids think you're doing?"

We turned to see principal Turner standing at the door.

"We were just—"

"Just what? Breaking into my office. Wait a second, weren't you all in detention?"

"We did but we just escaped. That monster trapped us in here."

"Trapped you—monster? What are you talking about?"

"The killer—"

"He has two faces and already killed Ms. Barnes and Mr. Perkins—"

"We need to get out of here!"

"Call the police!"

"Now just hang on a second," he said holding a hand up. He wasn't reacting the way we hoped at all.

He seemed annoyed, like this sort of thing has happened before.

He took a seat behind his desk. "Look, I don't have time for Halloween pranks. I already lost my keys, someone stole my pager, and now I have students running around claiming a killer is on the loose."

"If you don't believe us, try the phones—"

"That creep disconnected them all. We're telling the truth, try it!"

Mr. Turner gave us a suspicious look over, like a detective would a suspect. "If I pick up this phone, and hear the dial tone, you will serve detention all next week. Got it?"

"Just pick up the damn phone—" Billy said aggressively. "Er—I mean, please sir."

"Watch it." Mr. Turner, reluctantly, picked up his desk phone and raised it to his ear. At first nothing, but then his facial expression changed. His eyes went wide. "The phone line, its—"

"Dead! That's what were trying to tell you."

"He cut the phone lines and blocked all the entrances. The freak trapped us in here. We can't leave!"

"If you kids did something to the school's phone lines, that is more than a detention. You are looking at suspension."

"You got to be kidding me?"

"Go look at the dead bodies as proof. Go see the creepy mannequins in the theater."

"Bodies? Mannequins? Okay that's enough! You kids need to stop this ridiculous prank—"

Before he could finish his sentence, a loud boom echoed in the school, and all the lights went out. It was pitch black.

We all stood in his dark office, the only light coming from the setting sun outside, a mixture of gold and yellow barely sneaking through the storm clouds that were brewing outside.

The entire school had lost its power.

And now, in a few minutes, we'd be surrounded in total darkness.

"Do you believe us now?"

Chapter 11

Standing in total darkness, I couldn't tell who-was-who. People were moving and shifting. Emily was freaking out. Billy was trying to calm her down. Principal Turner was rummaging around at his desk.

Seconds later a beam of yellow light cut across the darkness.

He scanned the flashlight around the office, spotlighting us.

"I swear if you kids are responsible for this, you are in so much—"

"Give us some credit Mr. Turner. Do you really think we would choose to stay after school on Halloween night?"

"Yeah, why would we want to miss the Pumpkin Festival?" Reese pointed out. "And all that free pumpkin pie!"

"It does seem odd," Turner replied. "Regardless, it's probably just a flipped breaker from the storm. I'm going to look around, see if I can find the maintenance man. You kids should go home before this gets any worse."

"We already told you, we can't! That freak locked all the exits and sealed all the doors shut."

"Who did?"

"The killer!"

"That freak with two faces."

"Drama Freak!"

"I think you kids have been watching too many scary movies. For now, just stay here and I'll go check things out. Maybe I can find the maintenance man to get the backup generators on. But drop this whole killer on the loose thing, I've had enough Halloween tricks for one day." He shot Reese a glance. "Seriously."

Against our protesting, principal Turner left his office without another word.

We watched in silence as he made his way down the hall, his flashlight cut back and forth across the walls, and he turned around a corner and disappeared.

"What do we do now?" Emily said back up behind the desk.

"We wait for him to get back. No way I'm going out there, killer or no killer."

"If we stay here, we could be killed too. What are we supposed to do, hold up in this office until he's back?"

"Why not?"

"That's *if* he comes back."

"Hey, don't say that."

"Were all thinking it."

"Actually, I was thinking how we wouldn't even be in this mess if it wasn't for—"

"Enough Billy," I told him firmly. "Blaming Reese isn't going to help us now, and it certainly won't stop whoever is doing this. We need to figure out what's going on, we must do something."

"Agreed," said Marcus. "Even with this freak running around, we have to try something."

"What can we do?"

Billy, who was searching through drawers and other cabinets, finally pulled something out of a drawer. Two small, miniature flashlights. He pressed both on, and two beams of yellow cut across the room. He handed me the other flashlight. "Let's find a way out."

In the brief shell of light, I could see everyone's terrified facial expressions.

"You actually want to go out there?" Claire as Billy.

"I don't plan on sitting here doing nothing, waiting to die."

"So, you're going to what, fight the killer?" Reese asked.

"Not just me," he ushered to Marcus, who was pacing back and forth, hands on his head. "I figured we could take this psycho on, whoever they are."

"I don't know Billy, playing sports is one thing. This is a whole different ball game now."

"Oh, suck it up!" Billy said. "Or stay here if you want, I'm going to go look for principal Turner and help get this power on, so we can get out of here."

"Okay, so do we split up?"

"Yeah, let's just give the killer what he wants. Easier targets."

"At least it's just one killer." Marcus reminded us.

"That we know of," suggested Reese.

Everyone shot a weary glance at each other.

"Fine, we stick together and if we come across this Drama Freak, we take him head on. Six versus one, I like those odds."

"Agreed."

"And be on the lookout for any clues to who this might be." I said.

"Great advice detective."

"Okay, everyone ready?" I asked.

They all nodded.

And one by one, we left the front office and into the pitch-black halls of Hollow Creek High.

Chapter 12

We started walking down the main hallway leading from the front office.

We kept passing rows of red lockers, and darkened classrooms, which became illuminated with silver linings in between the lightening flashes.

Once we made it to the center hall of the main atrium, we stopped. We looked all over, but there was no sign of principal Turner, or anyone.

Before we could do anything else, upstairs a door closed.

We ran after the noise.

If it was the killer, we would take him on. All of us.

We rushed up the stairwell and burst into the second floor.

I shined my flashlight around the halls, into the classrooms, each one was completely empty. The circle of flashlight combed across the lockers, into the classrooms, and over the floors.

When the beam hit the floor up ahead, there was a sparkle of red, like a trail of rubies.

"Let me see that," I said grabbing the flashlight from Billy.

When I walked over and shined the light on the floor, dozens of blood drops peppered the hall, like scattered rubies falling out of a torn pocket.

Then the little spats of blood turned into bloody footprints leading around the corner up ahead.

"Look, footprints. Let's see where they lead."

They all looked down with wide eyes.

I started to follow the trail of red footprints down the hall.

"What are you doing?"

"We need to find out whose blood this is."

"What for?"

We turned the corner, and the bloody footprints turned into a small puddle, then a larger puddle, before coming to a pool of blood, with a pair of shoes in the middle.

I raised my light up, and standing in those shoes, in the pool of blood, was Principal Turner.

I reached out a hand.

"Principal Turner?"

My voice went ghost as his body went limp and fell to the ground.

A dark shadow emerged closer, and two white faces were staring at them among the pitch black.

One smiling. One frowning.

The two headed freak stepped forward and spoke in a raspy, shrill voice that sent goosebumps crawling down my back.

"Hello children! Allow me to introduce myself, I am Drama Freak, and I welcome you the main event."

The last thing I remember was everyone screaming and running off in different directions, disappearing into the school.

"This will be one killer Halloween!"

The raspy laughter of Drama Freak echoed behind us, sending goosebumps down my neck.

"HEHEHE-HEHE-HEH!!."

I ran and ran and didn't look back.

Chapter 13
Emily

Billy and Emily ran and ducked into a nearby storage closet. They sat their for a few minutes, waiting for the hall to go quiet.

"I think we're safe for now," said Billy, pressing his ear to the wooden door.

"Why did you have to kiss her?"

"What?"

"Why did you have to kiss Shelby? She was my best friend."

"Are you serious right now? You want to talk about that here?"

"We could die tonight, I want to know."

"I don't know why, but she definitely made the first move." Billy assured her.

"That's not what I heard."

"Who are you going to believe? Some girl who has always been jealous of you, or your boyfriend?"

"I don't know what to believe anymore..." Emily said turning away from him.

"But you invited the new kid over to your party, what's that all about?"

"I was just being friendly, welcoming him to the school."

"Well maybe if you weren't throwing yourself at every guy, trying to make me jealous, I wouldn't have kissed another girl. Just saying."

"Screw you Billy," she said shoving him aside and running out the closet and into the hallway.

"Where are you going?!"

"Away from you." She said, and ran into the nearest bathroom, locking the door.

He tried opening the door. No budge.

"Open the door Em, we need to stick together right now. Look, I'm sorry for what I did! I didn't mean it."

"Leave me alone Billy."

"Come on Em, just come out so we can talk."

"Billy, go away!"

"I'm not going to—"

Billy didn't finish his sentence.

The sound of his footsteps running away echoed down the hall.

It was quiet again.

Emily looked up from the sink, wiping her eyes. She stared into the mirror, her mascara running down with her tears. "B-b-Billy?"

No answer.

"Did you really just leave here me alone you jerk?"

Still no reply.

"Come on this isn't funny."

She went over to the door and listened to the other side. Silent.

She unlocked the door and stuck her head out into the hall.

"Billy?"

No one was there.

"Oh, we are so broken up."

She backed up in the bathroom, opened a stall and got inside quickly.

She leaned her head against the stall door and waited.

Then she noticed she was standing in something wet on the floor.

Gross, she thought. Someone pissed on the floor.

She took a step back and her foot hit something soft behind her.

She turned and saw a body lying in the stall.

Her eyes had adjusted to the darkness, and she was able to make out the dead body sitting on the toilet.

It was her friend, Shelby Wilson.

No wonder I didn't see her after class! She thought.

Her eyes were lifeless and bloody shot, her body limp, and her head leaned on her shoulder. Her neck was broken and swollen.

"Shelby?.."

Emily screamed, unlocked the door, ripped it open, and ran down the hall as fast as she could, tears streaming down her face.

She ran around a corner and stopped.

There was a figure at the end of the hall.

It was the—janitor!

He was standing with a mop and bucket, cleaning the floors.

"Help me! Please! They're all dead, and we need to get help and—"

She stopped running a few feet from where the janitor stood.

The janitor turned around and he wasn't holding the broom.

He was holding a long, squishy rope in his hands.

When the lightning flashed, in his hands, he was holding his own intestines.

Across his belly, a huge gash, wide open and spilling his guts.

He took a step towards her, then another, and fell to his knees, before falling into a bloody plop on the ground.

A raspy voice spoke from the side in a dark classroom.

"Are you okay?"

She slowly turned her head and two heads with white faces were staring at her.

Drama Freak was watching her.

The face with an evil smile spoke to her in that cold, raspy voice.

"He didn't have the guts for this performance."

Emily screamed into the night, running back into the darkness of the school.

Chapter 14

Billy

"That girl I swear."

Billy made his way down the science hall.

He figured he could take the east stairway to get to the gym. He figured his football coach would still be there. Or so he hoped.

He took a deep breath and dipped into the stairway. He ran downstairs two at a time, bounding down. He crashed hard and bolted out the stairway doors.

Stupid to make that much noise but he didn't care. He had to get out. He had to find help. He had to...

There was movement to his right. Down the hall. It looked like—

A large dark shadow moved in front of him and Drama Freak bounded towards him like a mad wraith, it's two white faces staring at him with black eyes. One smiling. One frowning.

"Hey—wait, wait, wait—oh crap!"

Billy turned and ran as fast as he could back the way he came. His athletics had never come in more clutch then right now.

Drama Freak was on his tail, but Billy quickly lost sight of him after turning a quick corner and diving into the nearest room, sliding behind the teachers desk.

Moments later Drama Freak came strolling by. Billy waited there, holding his breath, until he couldn't hear anything outside the room.

"Screw that freak."

Billy got up, peeked outside the doorway, and the coast was clear.

He ran out and made a dead run to the gymnasium.

Coach Mercer is probably still in his office, especially with the big game tomorrow. That was his best bet.

He bolted down the athletic hall and made his way past the gymnasium. He thought back to earlier when Reese was pelting him with dodgeballs. "I swear when we get out of this, I'm going to kill that kid."

He checked inside the locker room. The only light was coming from the other end, from the tiny ceiling windows.

Moonlight poured in, as rain continued to pelt the rooftop.

"Coach?" He whispered. "Coach, you in here?"

The coaches office door was wide open, and he saw a trail of blood leading out and away from the locker room.

"Coach?..." Billy peered his head inside and saw in horror the dead body of Coach Mills, sitting at his desk, with his head severed, resting beside him on the desk.

"Oh God…"

"Looks like he lost his head." A voice spoke from behind him.

Billy spun around to find Drama Freak staring at him. Those faces, one smiling and one frowning.

"You're a monster."

Billy ran for the door.

Drama Freak slung his arm out, extending his bladed fingers and slashing at Billy.

Red drops fell from the tips as Billy roared in pain. The bladed fingers left a large gash across his forearm as blood spilled to the ground.

"You got that right."

Drama Freak lunged again at Billy.

One of the blades slashed through his letterman jacket and he felt a hot, burning sensation as he looked down and saw blood pooling under his jacket, running down his shoulder.

Billy stumbled into the wall but kept his balance as he ran out of the locker room and back towards the gymnasium.

He ran over to the doors, out into the hall and the next time he looked back, Drama Freak was gone.

Chapter 15

Marcus

Marcus was always fast, but running from a two-headed killer, somehow gave him superhuman speed.

He ran so fast he found himself under the bleachers in the gymnasium without even realizing it.

"Man, this is seriously messed up," he whispered to himself. *"The one night all the freaks come out."*

He couldn't tell how long he was hiding.

Seconds, a minute or two. He didn't know.

The only sound he heard was the thumping of his heart in his chest.

His heart was beating so loudly it sounded like it was bouncing out of his chest and onto the gym floor.

Thump. Thump. Thump.

Wait. That's not my heart, he thought.

Thump. Thump. Thump.

It almost sounded like— *"Is that a basketball I hear?"* He thought out loud.

He peeked around the bottom of the bleachers to see where the sound was coming from.

Sure enough, it was a basketball.

Bouncing by itself in the middle of the basketball court.

After several more bounces, the basketball rolled a few feet and stopped.

Marcus walked over to the basketball and picked it up.

He looked around and didn't see anyone.

"Hello?"

Then he felt it. It was a gut feeling that someone was watching him.

He scanned the darkness of the bleachers, and at the very top he saw a dark robbed figure standing there. Two white faces watching him with evil smiles.

It was Drama Freak.

He was standing still, like a dark statue.

"What the—" Marcus took a step back. "You stay over there. You don't want to mess with me. I'm serious. I don't know who, or what you are, but I'm not playing with you."

Drama Freak didn't move or say a word.

Both faces seem to be fixed on Marcus.

He took a step to the left and the heads slowly shifted to him.

The faces seem to follow his every movement.

Like predator hunting its prey.

He could sense the tension in the air. As if any second—

Drama Freak shifted and exploded down the stairs at Marcus.

"Yo—YO CHILL OUT!" Marcus hollered as he turned and started running for his life. He made his way for the gymnasium doors.

He looked over his shoulder and Drama Freak was a couple feet away, gaining on him.

His long fingers reached out to grab his neck, but he dodged it at the last second. The sound of metal against metal rang in his ears.

Once he made it out to the halls, he turned several corners, nearly crashing into the lockers as he ran.

He dived into the nearest classroom. An art room.

But he wasn't alone.

Someone was already in here…

A figure moved in the shadows and out emerged Claire.

"Claire?!" Marcus sounded relieved and scared. "What are you doing here?"

"Hiding," she said. "From him."

Marcus turned to the doorway.

Long fingers slowly wrapped around the edge of the door, and two white faces emerged from the darkness.

Lightning flashed and Drama Freak stood hunched in the doorframe, his two faces staring at them with lifeless black eyes.

Marcus got in front of Claire and braced himself.

"Come on then Freak, come get some!" Marcus roared, holding up his fists.

From down the hall, a flashlight blasted the hallway and Drama Freak reared around and vanished out of sight into the darkness.

The light grew closer.

Someone appeared moments later, blinding him with light.

"Marcus? That you?" Billy asked, shining the beam of light into his face.

"Yeah, it's me. Mind lowering the light there for me."

"My bad," said Billy lowering the flashlight. "You guys, okay?"

"Okay as we'll ever be," said Claire, emerging from behind Marcus.

"Right," Billy checked out into the hall, "come on, let's go find those other two dweebs and find a way out of this hellhole."

Chapter 16
Reese

Reese ran down the hallway not looking back, not stopping until he found himself in the empty cafeteria.

The storm raged outside, and lightning flashed, casting a silver glow across the tables.

Normally it was bright and vibrant during the day. Now it was dark and filled with silent shadows.

He heard a rumbling noise.

His stomach.

He realized he hadn't eaten anything since lunch.

"Screw this, I'm not going to die on an empty stomach."

He entered the back kitchen, and started rummaging through the cabinets and pantries, looking for any kind of snacks to scavenge.

"None of this looks good. I wouldn't feed any of this to my dog."

He kept searching through frozen lasagnas, chicken tenders, French fries, and all things frozen.

"Great, guess I will die hungry."

"Try the other cabinet," a high raspy voice said behind him.

He turned to see Drama Freak standing in the kitchen across from him.

"Stay back freak, I'm warning you!"

"Come now Reese, don't you want to play with me?"

"I'm serious, I've seen all the movies, and I know how this goes."

Reese grabbed the nearest frying pan off the rack and held it to his face like a sword.

"What are you going to do?" The chilling, raspy voice spoke. *"Fry me an egg?"*

"No, I'll knock you upside your heads. I'm not scared of you."

Neither of the faces said anything. Just staring at him with empty black eyes.

Thunder boomed overhead and lightning flashed.

Reese shot a glance over his shoulder at the cafeteria area, and when he turned back, Drama Freak was gone.

Reese slowly backed up deeper into the kitchen, scanning every direction.

His eyes had already adjusted to the faint level of light, and years of sneaking downstairs past his bedtime had prepared him for just such an occasion.

There was no movement. No sound other than rain pelting the roof and windows.

Movement out the corner of his eye caught his attention. He raised the frying pan high, ready to strike, when a silver food can came rolling out of the darkness stopping at his feet.

He looked up into the darkness, and two faces were staring back at him.

Drama Freak lunged and sprinted towards him, bladed hands outstretched.

Reese sprang backwards over the kitchen tables, knocking all sorts of pots and pans to the ground. That bought him enough time to duck out the door as Drama Freak came slashing his long-bladed fingers, barely missing his face. He felt the wind brush his hair as the blades dug into the kitchen walls, leaving long scratches.

Once he was out the door, he ran down whichever way he could and ran faster than he had ever ran before.

Wow! He thought. *I'm just like the helpless victims in the movies I watch.*

He ran around corner after corner, ducking into a new hall with every turn. He checked only once over his shoulder, but nothing was chasing after him.

He was alone.

He crouched behind an empty corner, peeking around to see if the coast was clear.

Aside from the growing storm outside, the halls all seemed empty and quiet.

Something bright and flashy caught his eye.

Coming from the front of the school, he saw red and blue lights flashing, glazing the ground and rainy windows.

Is that a police car?

He gave a quick look over his shoulder once more, only to find an empty hall and dark classrooms.

Sweat was dripping off his forehead.

He slowly stood up, took one last peek behind him, and ran towards the flashing red and blue lights.

Chapter 17

When I saw the flashing red and blue lights I felt the biggest relief. Like a knight on a white horse had been sent to save us from this nightmare.

I ran towards the windows and watched as the officer got out of his police cruiser, turned his flashlight on, and started walking towards the school. He wore a dark blue poncho.

Rain blistered my view, but I knocked on the window repeatedly. I didn't want to yell, but maybe he could still hear the knocking from out there.

Knock. Knock. Knock.

The officer must have heard it because he shined his flashlight in my direction, and I was covered in pale-yellow.

He jogged over to the doors at the front entrance.

The officer tried opening the doors, but they didn't budge. He yanked and yanked but the doors were sealed and chained shut.

I ran over to him at the front doors. Rain plastered the glass as he approached.

I saw a flash of gold under his poncho.

A police badge with the last name "Mercer" engraved on it.

They won't open, I mouthed the words over and over until he understood.

"Can you open it from inside?!" He yelled over the rain.

No, no, no I mouthed.

"Is anyone hurt?!"

I shook my head up and down repeatedly *yes yes yes* but then I froze.

There was movement behind the officer. Lightning flashed and two white faces appeared behind officer Mercer.

"BEHIND YOU!" I screamed.

He shook his head. "What are you—"

Out of nowhere the officer's face exploded with blood as bits of flesh flung and stuck against the window. His face opened like a red flower, and sticking out of his face at different angles, the bladed hand of Drama Freak.

Bits of flesh and blood ran down the window, getting washed away by the rain.

The body of officer Mercer staggered, then crashed against the window and slowly left a bloody trail as his body slid against the window.

"No…"

No, no, no. This can't happen right now. I just watched our only hope of getting rescued get turned into a flesh flower.

Drama Freak stood there in the rain. Watching me. Tilting his head to each side, both faces studying me.

Then he backed away slowly.

He walked over to the police car, leaned in and turned the flashing red-and-blues off, turned the car off, then walked towards the back of the school and vanished out of sight into the heavy rain.

Chapter 18

Somewhere in the school a door opened. I didn't know where to go, so I started walking down the main hall, passing dark room after dark room, but the sound of approaching footsteps stopped me.

Footsteps heading for me and fast.

I was about to turn and hightail it when two hands wrapped around my mouth and dragged me into the nearest classroom.

Whoever this was, shoved me behind the teacher's desk and pulled me down.

I began to fight back when I heard a familiar voice whisper in my ear.

"Shut up."

I went silent as a statue as I heard the footsteps getting closer, coming down the hall.

My eyes finally adjusted to the dark, and Reese was staring back at me, eyes wide, holding a finger over his mouth. He motioned towards the door.

I kept quiet and peeked around the corner of the desk, staring out the door into the hall.

It was darkness, except for when lightning flashed.

Darkness. Flash. Darkness. Flash. Darkness.

On the next flash, a figure was standing in the doorway.

A figure in a dark cloak, with two faces.

I held my breath as Drama Freak scanned the room.

He stood there for a moment or two. Not moving. Just watching. Waiting.

I looked away, hoping at any second, I would wake up from this nightmare.

The sound of footsteps walking away faded into the school, and the room was silent as the night.

I held my breath, and the next time I looked back at the doorway, it was empty.

"I think he's gone," I whispered. *"Thanks for that."*

"Don't mention it," he replied quietly. "Now what do we do?"

I got up and walked over to the door and peeked into the hall. There wasn't a trace of anyone around.

"Come on, the coast is clear," I told him. "Let's get out of here and find the others."

Chapter 19

Once it was quiet again, we walked back out into the hallway. "Where are the others you think?"

"Don't know," I told him, looking back over my shoulder. "Hopefully they're still alive."

"So, who do you think it is?"

"What do you mean?" I asked him, having a slight suspicion of what he was asking.

"You've seen the movies. The cartoons. This has got to be someone behind all of this."

"Oh, well I haven't really thought about it too much."

Truth is, I haven't.

I've been too shocked to think about anything other than running and hiding for the past few hours.

"It's got to be someone who knows the school." I told him.

"What do you mean?"

"I can't put my finger on it, but it's almost as if Drama Freak knows where to find us. Like a way of knowing where we are."

"How so?"

"Well, remember when Drama Freak was looking in the rooms? It seemed like it always knew the classrooms it was searching."

"You're saying it's someone who works at the school?"

"Or goes to it."

"Either way, we need to find the others and figure out a plan to get out of here. I'm not dying in a high school."

Movement caught my eye in the classroom we just passed.

I turned and stared into the darkness.

The faint moonlight barely illuminated the desks and chairs, but when lightning flashed outside, the entire room and hall exploded with light, and I saw him. Hiding behind the doorframe, two faces staring back at me around the door.

"Looking for someone?" Drama Freak said in that raspy, sinister voice.

He lunged out of the classroom, long fingers reaching out to grab me. I nearly fell to the ground trying to run away. I barged into Reese, and we stumbled into a sprint down the hall.

"Is he still behind us?"

I turned to look, and Drama Freak came bursting around the corner, both faces staring into my soul.

"Y-yes! Keep running! Don't stop!"

We ran and ran, hallway after hallway, and just as we turned into the next hall, we ran into someone.

A familiar voice roared at me.

"Ow—what the hell is wrong with you?!"

I looked up to Billy and Marcus staggering up over us. Emily and Claire were running up behind them.

"Drama Freak—behind us—chasing…"

We were both out of breath, and my adrenaline was so spiked I felt like running on water.

"We must have lost him."

"Okay, this is too much." Reese said.

"Seriously, we need to get out of here." Marcus told me. "We stay here any longer, that Freak isn't going to stop until he hunts us all down."

"Maybe we could him hide out, and survive until dawn?" Claire wondered.

"How do we do that?"

"I say we go back to the library, barricade the doors, and wait it out." Emily suggested.

"Yeah, and that Freak will just come for us outside of school."

"What do you mean? You think he would he would still come for us?"

"Well, something about Drama Freak strikes me strange. It seems as if he's playing with us, like he knows who we are."

"So, you're saying we're his targets, why?"

"I don't know. That's the part I haven't figured out."

"Ok, so what? We just wait it out till morning, and someone will come to help us tomorrow?"

"I'm down for that." Said Marcus.

"Same here." Said Reese.

"If it's our best shot, then I'm with it." Billy said.

"No," I said. "We aren't going to do that."

"What?" Claire muttered.

"You got a death wish new kid?

"Are you saying we should just wonder the halls waiting for him to kill us?" Reese suggested, "You might as well ask him to go trick-or-treating with us too."

"Let's get back to the library." I said, looking at all of them. "I got a plan."

Chapter 20

"Wait, you want us to do what?" Marcus asked as we ran. We got back to the library in a group sprint. Emily held on to Billy. Claire stayed next to Marcus, and me and Reese ran up to the front.

The first thing we did entering the library was barricade the door with chairs and two tables.

"We should be good for now. Whoever this Freak is, no way he could get through this."

"Okay, so what's this plan of yours detective?" Billy said, stacking the last of the chairs against the barricaded pile.

"We plan the trap."

"What trap?"

"The one we're setting for Drama Freak."

"You want us to catch him?"

"How are we supposed to do that detective?" Billy asked.

Reese looked skeptical. "You guys seriously didn't watch Saturday morning cartoons did you?"

"No," said Billy, "some of us are popular and have friends."

"Exactly," I said. "We're going to set a trap, as ridiculous as it sounds, but it's our best shot."

"I still think we should wait it in here until the morning." Claire suggested.

"No way I'm waiting hours while this killer stalks us. Waiting for us." Billy said, and Marcus agreed.

"As long as he's out there, and we're in here, we should be safe." Claire suggested out the corner of her mouth.

"You really believe that?"

"How can he get to us?" She asked desperately.

"I don't know, but I'm not taking any chances. And I'm not giving that Freak any opportunity to escape. After tonight, after all the killing, we need to stop whoever this is and do it for the lives lost tonight."

"So, were basically going to capture a psychopath killer-demon?"

"Pretty much."

Everyone exchanged looks of worry.

All except Reese.

He seemed to be excited. I didn't blame him, it's not everyday you get chased around your high school by a freaky two-faced monster. Or maybe you do?

I'll admit, as much as I was scared too, I had to agree with Reese.

This is almost, in a weird way, *fun*.

Reese shot me with a grin. "Happy Halloween!"

Chapter 21

We gathered all the materials. Stacked chairs, books, a rope made of computer cords, and a blanket we found in Ms. Barnes office. I kept my eyes off her corpse as best as I could, but something about seeing a dead body in person shifts your perspective on life. This was once a living breathing person hours ago, now she was only a lifeless, bloody mass slumped in a chair.

After we had gathered all the materials, and got everything ready to go, we went over the plan one more time.

"This is it. We only have one shot at this. If we fail, some of us might not make it out alive tonight, but if we don't fail, we can save more lives from being killed, and avenge the others."

Marcus stepped up with a serious expression on his face. "Either we stop this monster right now, or we die trying."

"That seems a little extreme." Reese said.

"Seriously man? What about this night hasn't been?"

"Good point," I told him. "Now, let's go over it one more time."

I explained the plan again, accounting for every role and position.

"When Drama Freak rounds this corner, Emily and Claire you will be in opposite classrooms of each other, ready to pull the cord and trip him when he comes running around the corner. Once he trips over the cord, when he falls, Marcus and Billy, you two push the stacks of chairs so they fall on him, hopefully trapping him underneath. Then I'll run over, knock him in the head with one of these textbooks," I said holding up a biology book, "and with the blanket, we wrap him up, case closed."

"Seems way too easy."

"That's the point. If it's too elaborate, Drama Freak will know something is up. And like we said, if we don't do this now, who knows what will happen. Even if we survive the night, whoever is doing this—they can't get away and end up doing this to us again or worse, someone else. Drama Freak has already taken enough lives for one night. Now it's up to us."

Reese looked around at everyone. "Wait, what about me? What am I supposed to do?"

"Just like in the cartoons, you got the most important role of all."

"Don't tell me…"

"That's right, you're the bait."

"You're joking right?" He replied, backing away from us.

Emily rolled her eyes. "It's obviously the person whose fault it is were stuck in the mess in the first place."

All eyes fell on Reese.

"They got a point," I reminded him. "Besides, out of all of us, you've seen the most slasher films. If anyone can pull this off, it's you."

"Fine, I'll do it but not for you guys," he said looking at everyone but Alex. "I'm doing this because my only friend asked me to. Plus, I don't want my life in any of your bozo-hands."

"Okay, we all agree on the plan?"

Everyone looked around and nodded.

"Good," I said. "Time to catch a monster."

Chapter 22

Reese

"Great," Reese said to himself, walking down the dark hallway, passing lockers and empty classrooms. "Not only will I die tonight, but I get to die being the cheese in a mousetrap. Just great."

The halls were quiet.

Too quiet.

Reese slowly walked down the hallway, turned another, then another, until he was at the front of the school.

"Ohhh, Drama Freak! Come out come out wherever you are!"

No answer. Obviously.

It's not like a killer to alert you to his whereabouts, he thought to himself. "Better to just act like a helpless victim," he told himself. "That always draws them out."

So, Reese began wandering the school, with a terrified, helpless look on his face. Well, he wasn't helpless he thought, he was the bait after all, but terrified he was.

The hall seemed to grow darker.

His flashlight only a small circle of pale-yellow light, combing over the lockers and inside the classrooms.

He passed one classroom to his right and walked a few feet before he realized what he just saw.

A dark, cloaked figure standing in the doorway of the classroom.

It was Drama Freak.

"Come get me you—"

He didn't finish his sentence.

He wasn't talking to Drama Freak at all. But rather a tall mannequin with a black robe over it. The blank face of the mannequin was just as creepy though.

Do killers leave decoys? He thought and continued to walk down the hall.

Passing another classroom down on the left, he saw another tall, black robbed figure. It was another mannequin. He kept walking, the next classroom on his left, another tall, dark figure stood in the doorway. Another mannequin.

"Okay, this is wrong." He said to himself.

He turned into the next hallway and froze.

Over a dozen dark, robbed figures stood with their backs to him, staggered next to each other down the hall.

Then a sinister, raspy voice spoke from within the dark group of mannequins.

"Looking for me? Heh-heh."

"I'm not scared of you." A big lie.

There was no reply.

He started to approach the first dark robbed figure. He pushed the first mannequin over and revealed it's blank face staring up at him.

He kept walking.

He flashed the light into the next mannequin, and then the next, and just like the first, more blank face staring back at him.

He kept walking and checking each one.

Flashed the light, blank face. Light, blank face. Light, blank face.

He pushed another one, then another one, and another. All blank faces. All mannequins.

Only several dark figures left.

As he was inspecting the next closest one, behind it, among the others he still had to check, he saw a brief flutter of movement. It was almost as if a sudden breeze had ruffled the black robes.

He was here. He was sure of it.

He checked the next one, mannequin, another one, mannequin, and as he was about to reveal the next one; a chilling, raspy voice spoke from behind.

"Getting warmer."

He spun around to the last four figures, huddled close together, it was hard to tell if any of them were the real Drama Freak.

He shoved one of the last mannequins into the others and they all fell to the ground but one.

The last one stood there silently. But his shoulders were moving slightly up and down. Breathing.

Drama Freak spun around slashing the air with his long, bladed fingers, speaking in that high, raspy voice as he laughed. *"This is the part where you run."*

Chapter 23

Everyone was in place and the trap was set. Claire and Emily waited in opposite classrooms, ready to pull the cord. Billy and Marcus waited, ready to push the stacked chairs. And me with a blanket to throw over Drama Freak, wrapping him up.

All we needed was Reese to do his part and lure him back here.

Emily and Claire gave me a thumbs up. As Billy and Marcus did.

Everything was set.

A few minutes had passed and nothing yet.

The silence was starting to feel heavy around me. I kept checking over my shoulder every few seconds.

"Psst."

I turned to see Marcus sticking his head out of the classroom he was hiding in.

I shook my head like, *"What's up?"*

"What do we do if this doesn't work?" Marcus asked in a hush tone.

Honestly, I hadn't really thought about it. It's not like there was a plan B, so I said under my breath, "Improvise."

He nodded his head. *"Word."*

Emily and Claire stuck their heads out too.

"He's got this. Don't worry." I assured them quietly and waved them back to their spots.

As if on cue, I heard a scream coming from deep within the school.

Here we go.

I tried to make out what Reese was saying. It sounded like he was yelling, "HELP!" over and over.

It got louder and louder until a second later Reese came rounding around the corner, sliding, and started running straight towards me.

Emily and Claire knew to wait after Reese passed to raise the cord.

Reese passed by their doors, barely jumping across the cord lying on the ground.

Reese came barreling towards me, and behind him, nearly on his heels, was Drama Freak.

The two faces headed straight for me.

Drama Freak had both hands stretched out ready to grab us, with their long, bladed fingers slicing the air as he ran.

He was fast, faster than we anticipated.

When Drama Freak came across the cord—he didn't trip! I watched as the cord was half raised. Only one side had pulled it.

They missed their chance!

"Billy! Marcus! NOW!" I yelled down the hall.

From opposite classrooms, two stacks of chairs came rolling out, but they must have been too late because Drama Freak barged ahead, dodging the stacked chairs by an inch, still chasing after Reese…and now me!

I turned to run when I felt a bladed hand slash my back, digging into my skin like hot wires.

I yelled in pain but kept running.

I looked over my shoulder to see his two grinning white faces staring at me with those black, lifeless eyes.

The raspy voice spoke from behind me. *"Where do you think you're going Alex? You don't want to miss the encore."*

Chapter 24

"Reese don't stop! He's right behind us!" I peeked over my shoulder and Drama Freak was full speed after us. His bladed hands were reaching out for me. If I stopped for a second, he would wrap his long fingers around my neck.

"Take this next right," I hollered up at him. He was ahead of me by a few steps.

We took the next hallway on the right and headed towards the auditorium.

We made it to the auditorium and ran down the isles past all the red theater seats and ran backstage behind the big red stage curtain.

I whispered to Reese, *"Find a place to hide! Hurry!"*

In an instant, Reese flew behind some old props from the previous play. I hid behind a rack of old costumes, and not a second later, footsteps were on the wooden stage.

I peeked through the clothes as Drama Freak burst through the curtain.

The two white faces scanned the entire backstage.

When the masks fell on me, I ducked back behind the rack and held my breath.

The sound of my heart thumping in my chest was like a booming echo.

I was sure he would hear it.

He glided past the clothes rack. Scanning every inch.

He walked past the clothes rack and stopped.

I didn't realize it but when I got behind the clothes rack, one of the hangers was swinging back and forth.

I must have knocked it in the commotion.

Drama Freak slowly turned his faces to the rack.

I thought about running, but maybe if I kept extremely quiet and still—

A bladed hand crashed through the rack, barely missing my head.

I felt Reese grab my shoulder and pull me to my feet. "Just run!"

We bolted out the side exit door backstage and came bursting through the doors and down the hallway.

"Split up, he can't catch us both!"

We took different turns and ran down different hallways. I turned back to see if Drama Freak was still chasing me.

He wasn't there.

I crept up to the corner of the hall and peered around the corner.

Drama Freak lunged at me.

I fell backwards, sliding up against the lockers.

I looked up and saw two bladed hands stretching out to kill me.

It all happened so fast.

I thought I was dead, but when I looked up, Billy came charging from the side, dropping his shoulder and laying Drama Freak out. He crashed hard into the lockers and slumped to the ground.

He was trying to get up, but Marcus came out of nowhere and cracked Drama Freak upside the heads with a large textbook. His body went still and limp.

We all looked around…

"Did we get him?" Emily asked.

"We should tie him up before he comes to."

"Good idea, go grab the cord and we'll tie him up. Wait for the police to come and take care of—wait, shouldn't we unmask him to see who it is?"

"Obviously, this freak tried to kill us for the past six hours. I want to see the look on this person's face."

"Yeah, let's see who Drama Freak truly is."

They all looked at me.

"Alex, you should be the one to do the honors." Reese said, stepping aside.

I looked at everyone in the group.

We all had bloody cuts, and bruises. Billy had a mean gash across his forearm. Marcus has a busted eyebrow and lip. Emily clothes were bloody, and her hair was matted with dried blood. Bruises lined her legs. Claire had a cut across her cheek, but I don't remember when she got attacked.

I thought of the past several hours and what we had just endured.

What we had just survived.

What this person, this *maniac*, has put us through.

The lives lost tonight.

Whoever this is, they needed to face justice.

Drama Freak was starting to come to.

And the person behind the mask mumbled and groaned to himself, probably coming to realize his current situation.

He was caught. Trapped. This was it.

I reached under the two faces and slid my fingers down and under the flap of a thick mask. My knuckles brushed against bare skin. My stomach sank as I started to lift my hand up, pulling the mask off.

"Time to solve this mystery once and for all."

With a steady grip, I pulled the mask off in one motion and looked upon the true face of the monster staring back at me.

And I couldn't believe my eyes.

Chapter 25

"Mr. Perkins?!"
"Of course, it's the drama teacher!"
Yeah, it's me you little snot nosed brats," he snapped. Barely looking at any of us.

"But how?" I questioned. "We thought you were dead?"

"We saw your body!" Emily added.

Perkins smirked. "Of course you did, that's what I wanted you to see." His smile turned dark, and for the first time, I saw true evil gleam in his eyes. They seem to enlarge, like a predator watching prey.

"But why? Why do any of this?"

"Because..." He bit down hard on his jaw and spoke through gritted teeth, "Kids like you think you run high school. It was no different back in my day. The jocks and cheerleaders acted like kings and queens, while kids like me were bullied and outcasted for just being ourselves."

I saw Reese flinch at those last few words. Despite what Perkins had done tonight, I could tell Reese felt sympathy for his last statement. Reese considered himself an outcast who got bullied for being himself. They might not be that different...

I felt for Reese, and some part of me, deep down, felt bad for Mr. Perkins too.

"Why kill Mrs. Barnes, the librarian or the janitor? Or anyone?"

"I never killed the janitor, but the others were corrupt. Acting like good, hard-working citizens, when it was all them who were the biggest bullies in the first place. The principal, the football coach, the security guard, all of them were bullies. And I hate bullies. They disgust me."

"And your solution is to dress up in a freaky costume and kill them?"

"Well, that part was more for me," he said snickering to himself. "I can get a bit *theatrical* when I let loose."

"You son of a—" Billy lunged at Mr. Perkins and grabbed him by the collar. "You think this is funny you sicko?"

Mr. Perkins just laughed and smiled. Like he knew something we didn't. "Chasing you…stalking you…stabbing and slashing…it gives me such a, euphoric feeling…almost a kind of adrenaline…a *slasher high* if you will."

"My plan worked for the most part."

"Yeah, and now you're going to prison, congratulations loser." Emily said, spitting at him.

Reese knelt to eye level with him. "How were the others corrupt."

"We're all corrupt in some way." Perkins didn't look up at anyone. Instead, he stared at his feet, continuing to laugh to himself, like he knew a secret we didn't.

"Yeah well, now get to talk all about corruption to the police."

Chapter 26

Eventually the officers arrived. They managed to break down the front doors and when they found us, guns drawn, we quickly explained the situation and what had happened tonight.

"Officers, he's all yours." I told them as they placed handcuffs on his wrists and dragged him away.

Mr. Perkins looked over his shoulder at me and laughed hysterically.

"You haven't seen the last of us. Drama Freak will be back Alex Jones… we always come back."

Perkins roared with laughter as the officers shoved him down the hallway and out the front doors towards the police cruisers.

I didn't want to believe his words, but part of me knew something wasn't quite finished.

Somewhere deep down, I knew I would face Drama Freak again.

But what did he mean by *us*?

Billy stepped towards him and shouted. "Enjoy your alone time freak. I'm sure the padded cell will love to hear your stories."

With that, the last thing I saw of Mr. Perkins was the officer shoving his head down into the police cruiser, and slamming the door shut. When the taillights disappeared down the school drive, turning around the corner and out of sight, part of me felt relieved.

But another part of me felt like I missed something.

That's when an officer came walking out, carrying a box of personal stuff and papers, most likely evidence they found in his office.

When the officer left us, Reese snickered next to me.

"What?" I asked.

Reese held up a journal.

"What is that?"

"Just Mr. Perkins personal journal I swiped from evidence."

He opened it up and inside were various papers and drawings stuffed between the pages, which had neurotic scribbling all over it. School blueprints. Class schedules for each of us.

"Looks like he had been planning this for a while. This one is dated from last year."

I flipped through the papers, and saw diagrams and layouts of the school, class schedules for each of us, receipts for costume equipment: black hair wigs, custom face masks, dark robes and theater clothes.

"This must be his entire plan."

I opened the folded sketch paper and saw multiple drawings of Drama Freak and versions of his costume with different mask designs.

"Do any of these sketches look familiar to you"

"What do you mean?"

I studied the drawings. "There is something about these sketches, but I can't put my finger on it..."

"I can," said Marcus grabbing the journal. "They each have something in common, and we've seen it before." He took the sketches and held them up. "Take a closer look."

Then as I was scanning the papers, I noticed what was odd about the sketches.

We had seen this before.

Hours ago, in the library.

There was one thing each sketch of Drama Freak had in common.

They were all missing hands.

Chapter 27

"Wait, Claire went back inside to show the officer where you found Shelby's body?"

"Yeah, that's what I said." Emily replied, black mascara running down her face.

"Guess that means you're the most popular girl in school now Emily." Reese said raising an eyebrow.

"That's not funny Reese." She scowled at him, eyes brimming with tears.

"Oh, like you weren't thinking it."

"She was my best friend." She sobbed.

"Yeah, and thanks to Alex, if we didn't capture freak face we'd be just like her."

"Hold up," I was confused. "Emily, I—I don't remember you ever telling us where you found her body."

"Yeah okay, I guess I didn't so what? I had a lot going on tonight in case you haven't noticed."

"No, what I mean is—did you tell Claire?"

"No, are you kidding? She hasn't said a word since the police took Mr. Perkins away. After that she got all weird and quiet."

"Weird how?"

"She looked almost upset about the whole thing. Not scared or sad, but almost angry."

Of course, I thought. *Why didn't I see it before?*

"Everyone stay here," I said turning to face the school. "I'm going back inside."

"Wait, what?!"

"Why?"

"To solve this mystery once and for all."

"I'm coming with you," said Reese.

"No, I got this. If anything, you guys stay out here in case anyone tries to leave."

They all looked surprised, but no one objected.

"If I'm not back here in ten minutes, send help."

With that, I held up my flashlight to the front of the school and made my way back inside.

Chapter 28

I found myself walking through the front doors of the school. The high dark windows were staring down at me like black, lifeless eyes. I felt a dreading sense of unease as I opened the doors and stepped back inside.

"Okay now where did she go?"

I scanned the halls. No sign of movement. No sign of anyone.

I turned on my flashlight and started walking down the main hall.

Somewhere upstairs I heard a door open and close.

I ran to the nearest stairwell and bounded up the steps, two at once.

When I entered the second floor, I nearly slipped on the floor.

Catching myself, I shined my light down and saw bright red on the floor.

Blood.

Blood everywhere.

Bloody footprints trailed away down the hall and around the corner.

I slowly crept along the lockers, keeping the yellow circle of light on the bloody footprints.

Knowing that Mr. Perkins was arrested gave me some comfort, but something still wasn't right here.

When I turned the corner, my feet hit something on the ground.

I looked down and my stomach fell into an empty pit.

It was the officers bloodied body, perked up against the wall.

Shining the light at his face, his lower jaw had been torn off completely, bits of flesh dangled from his maxilla. Blood dripped into a tiny pool, forming on the floor between his legs.

I backed up and was about to run back to the others.

But I kept thinking, what happened to Claire?

At the end of the hallway, a flash of movement caught my eye.

A flash of pink and blue, and two white faces watching me, before disappearing into the darkness.

Someone yelled out from behind.

"Alex! What's going—"

Reese saw the officers body sitting in blood.

"Woah, wicked..." He got down closer and examined the corpse.

I shot him with a raised brow.

"What? Dude, this is like, straight out of a horror movie..."

I didn't respond. I was still trying to figure it all out.

Why would she do this? I thought to myself.

"Hey where's Claire?" Reese asked looking around the hallway.

I was too busy staring at the message written in blood on the wall.

Three large words written in blood, the letters leaking down to the floor in thin red streams.

DF WILL RETURN…

This definitely wasn't over, but for now, the mystery of Drama Freak was solved, the killer was unmasked, and all I wanted now, was to do was go home and take a hot shower. To wash this night off, along with the dried blood on my clothes and under my fingernails.

I turned back to Reese.

"What should we do now?" He asked.

I thought about it for a second.

"Honestly, I think the police can handle it from here. And I'm too tired to think about what's next."

His eyes lit up. "Pretty crazy Halloween huh?"

I looked at him and smiled.

This has been one big night of murder, mystery, and mayhem, I thought to myself.

I chuckled.

Of course it happened on Halloween.

Discussion Questions

1. If you were given detention on Halloween, how would you feel?
2. How would you defeat Drama Freak?
3. Would you stay in the library the entire night hiding, or would you try and find a way out?
4. What was your favorite part of the story? Who is your favorite character? Your least favorite?
5. If you had to guess, what would you predict for the plot of Slasher High 2?

About the Author

Jordan Stramer is the author of ***Slasher High***, his debut novel. Along with his writing, he has acting experience in film and television, including *Devotion*, *Legacies,* and *Stranger Things*. In his free time, he enjoys storytelling, exploring the world, and spending time with his family. Some of his life experiences include raising a German Sheperd named Vader, discovering a WWII bunker in Bermuda, and teaching himself to read and speak Korean.

Jordan was born and raised in Virginia.

Fun Facts: Jordan's favorite show is *Avatar TLA*, and his favorite book is *Wolf Brother*.

Creative Wisdom: *"Don't create a story the world needs, create a story you need."* -J.S.

Acknowledgments

Thank you for reading my debut novel.
This is ONE of many to come.
I have many stories in the works, and I look forward to showing you
all the magical worlds I've created...
1/100
-J.S.